The AUDIO FILES

by Tracey West

Illustrated by Rich Harrington

ISBN 0-439-90719-5
Copyright © 2006 by Scholastic, Inc.

Design by Kim Sonsky
Crime scene illustrations by Yancey Labat

12 11 10 9 8 7 6 5 4 3 2 1   6 7 8 9 1/0
Printed in the U.S.A.
First Printing, October 2006

Table of Contents

In the Mood for a Mystery?

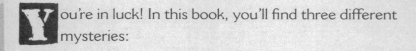

You're in luck! In this book, you'll find three different mysteries:

CASE #1

The Case of the Disappearing Dog: A prize-winning show dog is missing the night before the big competition! Can you figure out who stole Daisy, one of the top contenders to win Best in Show?

CASE #2

The Ghost of Wembley Manor: Is there a spooky specter in the manor, or is someone trying to scare Mrs. Wembley—to death?

CASE #3

The Case of the Super-Fried Hard Drive: A hotshot video game designer loses everything when his computer crashes. Did somebody sabotage him on purpose?

The best thing about these mysteries is that you get to solve them yourself! That's right. Find out what it's like to be a case-cracking detective and see if you can figure out the solution to each mystery. Here's how:

- **Keep track of the clues**: In each mystery, you'll find clues that point to suspects and their motives. Write them down in the notepad that came in your detective kit so you can refer back to them when it's time to solve the crime.

- **Study the crime scene**: In your kit, you'll also find photos taken at each crime scene. These photos show important evidence, so study them carefully.

- **Listen to the CD**: Each *You-Solve-It! Mysteries* book comes with tools that you can use to solve the crime. In this pack, you'll find an audio CD with sound recordings from each mystery. Each track contains clues to the case. Read each mystery, and then listen to the CD to see if you can crack the case.

When you think you've solved all the cases, visit the U-Solve-It! web site at **www.scholastic.com/usolveit** to check your answers. Just bring along this password:

SOUNDSLEUTH

The Case of the Disappearing Dog

FRIDAY, AUGUST 1
9:25 P.M.

"How does it feel to have a winning dog?"

Lisa Miller smiled at the reporter. "It's great! My family has been handling other people's dogs for years. This is the first time we've had a dog of our own in the show. We all knew Daisy could be a winner!"

Twelve-year-old Casey Miller stood on the side, away from the reporters, and watched her sister. Lisa held Daisy in her arms. The little Chihuahua shivered nervously.

I wonder if Daisy even knows she won? Casey mused. Casey almost couldn't believe it herself. She had been thrilled when Lisa asked her to come to the dog show to help out. She had helped her sister and her parents train, groom, and show dogs since she could remember. Now that Lisa was in college, her parents had trusted her with Daisy, their own dog. Lisa had devoted all of her spare time to making Daisy into the prizewinner she had become.

7

The Westburg Dog Show was one of the biggest in the country. Casey knew Daisy was an amazing dog. But she never dreamed Daisy would win her group. Lisa's hard work had paid off.

Casey felt a tap on her shoulder. She turned to see a boy with dark hair and brown eyes. It was Mike Simmons. His older brother, Alex, was a radio reporter who always covered dog shows. Casey and Mike only saw each other at shows a few times a year, but they had become friends.

"Congratulations," Mike said. "I think Daisy's going to go all the way. Best in Show, for sure."

"Best in Show?" It sounded too good to be true. "That would be awesome!"

"That's the word in the newsroom," Mike said. "It looks like Daisy's got a good chance. Her biggest competition is in the Working Group."

Casey nodded. In the dog show, each dog first competed with other dogs in its breed. Then the winner of each breed competed with other dogs in its group—the Toy Group (Daisy's group), Sporting, Non-Sporting, Herding, Working, and Terrier. Casey had seen some of the Working Dogs compete, and they were all beautiful, large dogs.

"It'll be fun to see Daisy go up against the big boys," Casey said.

Lisa walked up to them. "Hi, Mike," she said.

"Hey, Lisa," Mike replied. He gently scratched the top of Daisy's head. "Good job, Daisy!"

Lisa handed the little dog to Casey. "Case, I've got to do more of these interviews, but Daisy's frazzled. Do you think you could take her back to her crate until I'm done?"

"No problem," Casey said. She rubbed the Chihuahua behind her ears. "Come on, Daisy. I'll get you away from all this noise."

"See you tomorrow?" Mike asked. "I know the Best in Show competition isn't until Sunday."

"We'll be here tomorrow," Casey assured him. "We've got to check out the competition. Right, Daisy?"

Daisy just shivered in response.

Casey carried the dog through the maze of hallways underneath the sports arena where the dog show was held. She stopped in front of a door marked with a paper sign that read TOY GROUP. A uniformed security guard stood by the door. Casey flashed the official pass that hung on a cord around her neck, and the guard nodded for her to go in.

The room was deserted.

"I'll bet everyone's already at the first night party, right, Daisy?" Casey asked out loud. Every year, the dog show hosted a big party for dogs and their owners on the first night of competition. "I don't know if Lisa will take you. You need your rest for Sunday."

Casey opened Daisy's crate with one hand and placed the little dog inside. She took a small brush hanging outside the crate and began to brush Daisy's light brown coat. The Chihuahua closed her eyes, obviously enjoying the attention.

Casey sighed happily. When it came down to it, this was her favorite thing about dog shows. It wasn't the ribbons, or the parties, or the attention. It was taking care of the dogs.

Suddenly, Daisy erupted in a series of high-pitched barks. *Yip! Yip! Yip!* Casey turned to the door to see a black-haired woman in the doorway—Janet Kim, who handled a Shi Tzu, another dog in the Toy Group.

"Casey! Thank goodness! Blossom's on the loose!" Janet wailed, her voice full of worry. "She's running around the hallways here. Can you help me corner her?"

"Sure," Casey replied. She quickly closed the door to the crate and hung the brush back on its hook. Then she ran toward Janet.

Janet led her down a long hallway, then stopped. A high-pitched bark came from the corridor on the right.

"Let's go!" Casey cried.

Casey and Janet charged down the hallway. Blossom ran ahead of them frantically, turning corners faster than they could run. Finally, after fifteen exhausting minutes, Casey and Janet chased Blossom to a dead end. Janet scooped the shaggy little white dog in her arms.

"Bad girl, Blossom!" Janet scolded. "I'm taking you back to the party."

She turned to Casey. "Thanks so much, Casey. And congratulations about Daisy."

"Daisy!" Casey cried. If Lisa knew Casey had left Daisy all alone, she'd be furious. "Gotta run!"

Casey ran through the maze of hallways until she reached the Toy Group room. She ran inside. Then she gasped.

The door to Daisy's crate was open. Daisy was nowhere in sight.

Casey's heart started pounding, and she felt frozen in

place. It didn't make sense. Casey had closed the crate door before she left to help Janet, hadn't she? Daisy couldn't get out of the crate on her own.

It must have been Lisa, Casey realized. She took a deep breath. *Lisa has her. She's probably mad at me, but at least Daisy is safe.*

Casey and her sister both had red hair, green eyes, and freckles. Although they looked alike, Casey sometimes felt they were too different to be sisters. Lisa got straight As in school, kept her room clean, and never made mistakes. Casey, on the other hand, always seemed to be getting into trouble.

Lisa has Daisy, Casey assured herself. *There's nothing to worry about.*

But just then, Lisa walked into the room.

"Casey, where's Daisy?" she asked.

Casey slowly turned to face her sister. "You mean you don't have her?"

Lisa turned pale. "Oh, Case," she said. "What have you done?"

FRIDAY, AUGUST 1
11:45 P.M.

Casey's legs ached, and she felt like she could barely keep her eyes open. Once Lisa realized Daisy was gone, the two sisters had searched every inch of the sports arena looking for her.

First, though, they had reported the missing dog to the security staff. Dan Federman, the guard stationed by the Toy Group room, said he hadn't seen anyone come or go from the room. Everyone agreed that Daisy must have escaped from her crate.

"But I know I latched the door! I know I did!" Casey protested.

Lisa bit her lower lip. "Maybe you thought you did, Case. But the latch musn't have closed. You said you were in a hurry to help Janet, right?"

Casey's eyes filled with tears. "I always close the latch. I'm sure I closed it."

"It's okay, Casey," Lisa said, but her voice sounded flat. "We'll find her."

But even after hours of searching, there was no sign of Daisy. Casey and Lisa sank to the floor, exhausted. Dan Federman found them slumped against a wall.

"Sorry about your dog," the security guard said. "But we've got to close the arena now. She's probably just hiding somewhere safe. I bet she'll turn up tomorrow."

Lisa wiped her tear-stained face. "I hope so," she said weakly. Then she got to her feet. "Come on, Casey. Let's go back to the hotel."

Casey wearily stood up. She wished Dan was right. But somehow she knew he wasn't. She *knew* she had latched that crate, and that could only mean one thing.

Someone had stolen Daisy.

Casey walked across the street from the hotel to the arena where the dog show was being held. She had woken up extra early and thrown on a pair of jeans and a T-shirt. Luckily, her sister Lisa didn't wake up.

Casey had left a note for her and then quietly slipped out.

Lisa,
I went to the arena to find Daisy.
I am pretty sure someone took her.
I will find out who did it. I promise!

Love,
Casey

When Casey reached the arena entrance, she found Mike and his brother Alex there, pulling a cart loaded with sound equipment.

Alex noticed her before she could say hello. He whipped out a small notebook and paper from his pocket.

"Hey, Casey, is it true about Daisy? Did she really escape?" he asked.

Casey groaned. The news about Daisy had gotten out

quicker than she had hoped. She could just see the headlines now:

CASEY MILLER LEAVES LATCH OPEN ON CRATE! SHOW DOG CHAMPION ESCAPES!

"I don't think she escaped," Casey said. "I think someone stole her."

Alex frowned. He flipped through his notebook. "But the security guard said nobody went into the room after you left."

Casey's face flushed. She had forgotten about that. "Maybe he wasn't paying attention. I don't know. I just know that Daisy didn't get out of her crate by herself."

"Hey, Alex, quit bugging Casey," Mike said.

Alex shrugged. "I'm just trying to get the story. If we let the public know Daisy's missing, maybe someone will find her."

Alex picked up the handle of the cart and started to walk through the doors. He paused and turned to his brother. "You coming?" he asked Mike.

"I'll catch up with you later," Mike said.

Casey sighed. "So does everyone think I let Daisy get loose?" she asked.

"Word got around at the party last night," Mike said. "Most people feel bad for you guys. But your competition was pretty happy. Jason Temple said that maybe now some of the other dogs would have a chance to win."

"That's mean," Casey said. She didn't know Jason that well, but she knew he handled a Newfoundland, a big dog with black fur that would be competing in the Working Group later that day.

"So you really think someone stole her?" Mike asked.

Casey nodded. "It's just a feeling, but I'm sure I'm right. Now I've just got to prove it."

"How are you going to do that?" Mike asked.

"I'm not sure," Casey admitted. "I thought I'd sort of . . . look around. See if I find anything suspicious."

Mike's dark eyes shone with interest. "Can I help?"

"Sure," Casey replied. *Why not? Two heads were better than one, weren't they?*

> SATURDAY, AUGUST 2
> 7:45 A.M.

Casey and Mike walked down the hallways toward the rooms where the dogs got ready for the show.

"So, where should we start?" Mike asked.

"The Toy Group room," Casey said. "I want to check that latch myself. Maybe it's broken or something."

Mike nodded. "Good idea."

A security guard stood by the door of the Toy Group room, but Casey didn't recognize him. She and Mike showed their passes and opened the door. Mike stopped and put his arm in front of Casey.

"Wait," he said. "This could be a crime scene, right? We should be careful not to disturb anything."

He took a camera from his backpack and snapped a picture of the room.

Casey walked right to Daisy's crate. The door had been left open in yesterday's confusion. She closed it, and the latch automatically clicked in place—just like it always did.

"The latch is fine," Casey said. "No way did Daisy get out on her own."

"Maybe she's been practicing," Mike joked. "Like Houdini or something."

"Ha, ha," Casey replied, in a voice that clearly showed she did not think the remark was funny. "Hey, what's this?"

A long, straight, black hair was stuck in the wired walls of the crate. Casey pulled it out.

"That's weird," she remarked. "Daisy's hair is light brown."

"Save it!" Mike said. "Maybe it's a clue."

Casey had brought her backpack, too. She rummaged through the mess inside it and took out a plastic bag that had a few chocolate chip cookies. She dumped the cookies into the bottom of her backpack and put the hair in the bag. Then she sealed it up.

If it was a clue, what did it mean? That whoever took Daisy had black hair? It didn't even look human, really. More like dog hair . . .

Mike slowly walked around the room, taking pictures. He stopped suddenly in front of a crate near the front door.

"Hey, Case, come check this out," he called out.

Casey walked up to him. Mike pointed at the floor, where someone—probably someone grooming their dog—had spilled white powder on the floor.

"Grooming powder," Casey said. "Lots of groomers use it."

"But there's something inside the powder," Mike pointed out.

Casey looked more closely. A large paw print was just visible inside the dusting of powder.

"Yeah, it's a paw print. This is a dog show, remember?" Casey said.

"But it's a really *big* paw print," Mike pointed out. "None of the toy dogs made this print."

Casey and Mike looked at each other. "The Working Group!" they both said at the same time. The dogs in that group were some of the biggest in the show.

Then Casey frowned. "So, what does this mean? That a dog came in and stole Daisy?"

"Or someone came in with their dog," Mike said. He snapped a picture of the paw print.

"The working dogs should be getting ready for the show

in a few hours," Casey said. "Maybe we should go check it out. See if anything looks suspicious."

"Good idea," Mike said. "First, let's make sure we didn't miss anything in this room."

Casey and Mike walked around the room again. There wasn't much to see, really. Casey started to feel discouraged. So they had found a hair and a paw print—at a dog show. Big deal! A note from the guilty party would have been nice. *Hey, I borrowed your dog Daisy for a while. Meet me in the lobby and you can have her back whenever you want. Sincerely, The Dog Thief.*

Casey was about to call the search quits when she saw something shiny in a corner of the room. She walked over and picked it up.

It was a metal button, the kind you pin on your jacket to make a statement. This one was white with a brown paw print on it. Over the paw print were the letters PADS.

"Great," Casey said. "A button with a paw print on it. This could belong to anybody here."

"Save it anyway," Mike suggested. "You never know."

Casey slipped the

button inside the plastic bag with the hair. "What now?" she asked Mike. "This is starting to seem like a silly idea."

Mike looked at his watch. "Let's meet at the Working Group room around eleven o'clock. The dogs and their owners should be there by then. In the meantime, I'll ask around, see if anybody saw anything."

"Good idea," Casey said. "See you at eleven."

SATURDAY, AUGUST 2
10:42 A.M.

After leaving Mike, Casey had spent the next couple of hours walking around the arena. Dog owners were arriving early to get their dogs ready for the show. It had not been easy talking to people. Everyone seemed to know about Daisy, and they all asked Casey about what had happened. Casey had felt embarrassed every time she had to tell the story.

She didn't get much information in return. During the time that Daisy had been taken, everybody had been at the big party in the arena's restaurant. It had been crowded and noisy in there. Nobody had noticed anything strange.

Discouraged, and tired of answering questions, Casey had gone back to the Toy Group room. She sat down in the chair next to Daisy's crate. As she stared at the latch, she began to doubt herself.

What if I didn't close the latch? she wondered. *Maybe*

everyone is right. I should be looking for Daisy instead of some phantom dog thief. I should . . .

Exhausted, Casey fell asleep in her chair. She awoke awhile later to find Lisa shaking her shoulders.

"Casey, you shouldn't have left the hotel like that!" Lisa scolded. Her eyes were red from crying. "I already lost a dog. I don't want to lose a sister, too."

"I'm sorry," Casey said, yawning. "I just—I need you to believe that I didn't leave the door open. I have to prove that somebody took Daisy."

Lisa sighed. "You don't have to prove anything, Case. Accidents happen. I'm not mad at you. I just want to find Daisy."

She pulled a stack of flyers from the tote bag on her shoulder.

"I went to a copy place this morning," she said. "I've been putting posters up everywhere. Maybe you can put some up, too."

Casey looked at the flyer. There was a picture of Daisy, and a phone number so someone could call Lisa if they found her.

"That's nice," Casey said flatly. She knew it meant that Lisa still thought Daisy escaped.

"It wasn't easy," Lisa replied. "Somebody else has already papered the whole place with another flyer. Just look at this."

Lisa handed Casey a flyer that she had ripped off of a wall. It was a white flyer with a big brown paw print in the background. A message was printed over the paw print.

Casey felt wide awake. PADS—that was the logo on the button she had found. What if this anti-dog show group was somehow responsible for Daisy's disappearance?

DOG SHOWS ARE CRUEL TO DOGS!

DOGS SHOULD PLAY, NOT PRIMP!

HIGH PRESSURE SHOWS HARM DOGS!

—JOIN PADS— PEOPLE AGAINST DOG SHOWS

"Can I keep this?" Casey asked.

"Sure," Lisa replied. "You're not going to join or something, are you?"

"I'll explain later," she said. She looked at the clock on the wall. It was almost eleven. "I've got to run."

"You're going to put up those flyers, right?" Lisa asked. "Here, take this roll of tape, too."

Casey quickly stuffed the flyers and tape into her backpack. "Yeah," she said, but she didn't really mean it. She was anxious to talk to Mike.

Maybe they could figure this out after all!

Mike was waiting for Casey outside the Working Group room.

"I didn't find out much," Mike said. "Everybody was at the party last night."

"That's pretty much what I heard," Casey said. "But then Lisa showed me this." She took the PADS flyer from her backpack.

"Hey, isn't that the same group that's on the button you found?" Mike asked.

Casey nodded. "This group is against dog shows. Maybe they took Daisy to make a statement."

Mike looked thoughtful. "Maybe. But wouldn't they have left a note or something?"

Casey hadn't thought of that. "Who knows what a wacky group like that would do, right? I think we should look into it. Your brother has his laptop with him, right?"

"Yeah," Mike said.

"There's a web site on the bottom of the flyer. Maybe you can check it out," she suggested.

"Good idea," Mike said. "I'll do it when we're done here."

Casey and Mike walked inside the Working Group room. Dog handlers and owners bustled around the room, getting their dogs ready for the upcoming competition.

The dogs in the Working Group were giants compared to the tiny dogs in the Toy Group. Looking around the room, Casey saw a Doberman pinscher, a Saint Bernard, a Great Dane, and several other large dogs.

"These dogs are huge," Mike said. "The paw print we found could have belonged to any of them."

"Too bad we can't take their prints with an ink pad," Casey joked.

"Yeah, I don't think that idea would go over so well," Mike agreed.

Then Casey remembered something. "The hair!"

Casey took the plastic bag from her backpack. She held it up to the light.

"This had to come from a dog with long, straight hair," Casey said.

"I get it," Mike said. "If the paw print and hair came from the same dog, we could narrow it down to just a few dogs."

Casey scanned the room. The first black dog that caught her eye was a Burmese Mountain Dog, a large dog with a shaggy coat. Black hair covered its back and legs, but its chest and most of its face was white, with some brown mixed in on its head. A tall, thin woman with blonde hair brushed the dog's coat. She wore a business-like blue suit with a white blouse.

Casey tapped Mike on the shoulder. "Isn't that dog

called Reggie? He won Best in Show for the last two years.

"That's right," Mike agreed. "And that's Georgia Faller. She owns a bunch of dogs, but Reggie's the only one she always handles herself."

"Let's go talk to her," Casey said.

The two friends approached Georgia and Reggie. The dog greeted them with a deep, low bark.

"Please don't get too close to Reggie," Georgia said coldly. "He's got to go on in front of the judges soon. I don't want him upset. He's going for his third Best in Show win."

"He's favored to win, isn't he?" Casey asked.

"Yes, although not everyone seems to think so," Georgia said. "Imagine, thinking a scrawny little Chihuahua could take Best in Show from my Reggie."

"That scrawny little Chihuahua is my dog," Casey said, suddenly disliking Georgia Faller very much.

Mike quickly stepped between them. "We're just wondering if anyone saw anything last night, when Daisy went missing."

Georgia frowned. "Of course not. Reggie and I went to the party and left early so we could get our beauty sleep."

"You'll need more than beauty sleep to beat me, Georgia."

A tall, good-looking man walked up to them, with a black Newfoundland dog on a leash. Casey recognized Jason

Temple. She almost smiled at him, until she remembered what Mike had told her the night before. Hadn't Jason said he was happy that Daisy was out of the competition?

"Really, Jason, your Arthur is just a pup," Georgia said, her tone cold. "This is Reggie's year. Nothing is going to stop us. Especially not that scruffy Newfie of yours."

Casey looked at Jason's dog, Arthur. The dog had a beautiful, glossy coat of long, black hair. He didn't look scruffy at all.

"You're just jealous, Georgia," Jason said. "Reggie can't win every year. He's getting a little old for that, don't you think?"

But Georgia just smiled confidently. "We'll see, Jason. We'll see."

Casey tugged on Mike's sleeve. "Let's get out of here," she whispered.

They walked out into the hallway. Mike showed Casey two photos he had taken of Reggie and Arthur.

"So we found two dogs with long, straight, black hair and big paws," Mike said. "Do you think Jason or Georgia could have stolen Daisy?"

"Maybe," Casey said. "With Daisy out of the way, one of their dogs could win Best in Show. I always thought Jason was nice, but he did say he was glad Daisy was missing, right?"

"He was just being honest, I think," Mike said. "That Georgia seems pretty nasty. I could just see her stealing Daisy so that her precious Reggie wins the show."

"Me, too," Casey agreed.

"We'd better keep an eye on them both," Mike said. "The show starts at one o'clock."

"Sounds good," Casey said. "In the meantime, can you look up that web site for me?"

"No problem," Mike replied. "I'll meet you in the food court at noon, all right?"

"See you then," Casey said. She wasn't sure if they had found out anything that would help Daisy. *But it was better than nothing, wasn't it?*

Casey hung the flyers that Lisa had given her around the arena. Like Lisa, she found lots of PADS posters everywhere. She just covered them up with the Daisy flyers.

Then Casey headed to the food court on the third level of the arena to meet with Mike. The arena was crowded with dog lovers who had come to see the second day of competition. Casey rode the escalator to the third floor. On the escalator going down, she saw Jason Temple. He was standing next to Janet Kim. Casey was about to ask Janet how Blossom was doing after the big chase last night. But then she noticed that Jason and Janet were holding hands— and then Jason bent down and kissed Janet.

I didn't know they were a couple, Casey mused. Then a thought raced through Casey's mind faster than a runaway dog. *Jason . . . and Janet. She had to find Mike!*

Casey reached the top of the escalator and then impatiently pushed her way through the crowds of people who were trying to grab a hot dog or pizza before the show started. She scanned around and finally saw Mike, sitting alone at a small table in the corner. He spotted her, too, and waved her over.

"I got you some pizza," he said, pushing a paper plate and cup of soda in front of her.

Casey sat down across from him. "Thanks," she said.

"Guess what I just saw? Jason Temple and Janet Kim. Kissing. They're going out."

"So what? Are you jealous or something?" Mike asked, confused.

"No!" Casey said. "Don't you get it? Janet's dog lost to Daisy in the Toy Group. Maybe she wants to see Jason's dog beat Daisy. So she distracts me with a runaway dog . . ."

"And then Jason slips in, steals Daisy, and walks out!" Mike said. "That's brilliant! Except—"

"Except what?" Casey asked.

"That security guard didn't see anyone go in the room, right?" Mike said.

Casey sighed. "Maybe he wasn't paying attention. Anyway, it's the best idea we've got, right?"

"Probably," Mike said. "I checked out that web site, but I didn't find anything that will help."

Mike handed Casey a folder with papers inside. Casey took a bite of her pizza and looked through them. It was a bunch of stuff from the PADS web site, all about how dog shows were unfair because dogs didn't need extra stress in their lives.

"These guys don't know much about dog shows," Casey said, shaking her head. "Show dogs get treated great by their owners. All the dogs I know love the spotlight. It makes them really happy. Daisy especially . . ." Her voice trailed as she thought about the missing dog. It suddenly hit her that she might never see Daisy again. She almost started to cry.

Now cut it out! she told herself. *I've got to keep trying. I'll find Daisy. I can just feel it.*

She cleared her throat and shuffled through the papers again. "So who runs this thing, anyway?" she asked.

"There's a list in there somewhere," Mike told her.

Casey looked until she found a box with a list of names of people who worked for PADS. She read down the list—and one name popped out at her.

"Dan Federman!" Casey stood up, nearly knocking over her soda.

"Dan who?" Mike asked.

"Dan Federman," Casey said. "The security guard. The guy who didn't see anyone come or go."

Mike's eyes widened. "Because he was stealing Daisy himself!"

Casey grabbed the papers. "Let's go talk to him!"

Mike looked down at his plate. "Can't I finish my pizza?"

Casey nervously tapped her foot on the floor. "Okay. But hurry!"

SATURDAY, AUGUST 2
12:23 P.M.

The two friends wolfed down their pizza and then headed to the lower floor of the arena. Mike huffed and puffed behind her as Casey charged ahead.

"Don't come right out and accuse Dan," Mike called after her. "We've got to play it cool. Get him to confess."

"Whatever," Casey called back. She just knew Dan Federman had stolen Daisy and she wanted her dog back— now.

The Toy Group competition was over, so Casey wasn't sure exactly where she'd find Dan. She ran through the hallways, hoping he had been given a new assignment. After a few minutes, she found him stationed in front of an elevator.

"What did you do with Daisy?" Casey blurted out.

"What?" Dan asked.

"I know who you really are," she said. "You're with that group PADS. You stole Daisy as a protest or something. That's why you didn't see anyone go in or out of the room when I left. Because you took Daisy yourself!"

"I didn't take Daisy, I swear!" Dan said. "She was a sweet little dog. I wouldn't do that. I *like* dogs. That's why I'm in PADS."

"So how come you didn't see anyone go in or out?" Casey asked.

Dan sighed and looked down at his shiny black shoes. "I'm sorry," he said. "I only took this job so I would have access to the arena. So I could put up my flyers. After you went in the room with Daisy, I snuck off to put up some flyers. When I got back to my post, you were already going crazy looking for her."

Casey stared at him. "Why should I believe you?"

"I can't prove it," Dan said. "I just hope you can believe me."

Casey turned to Mike. "What do you think?"

"It makes sense," Mike said. "Maybe your idea about Jason was better. It's too much of a coincidence that he and Janet Kim are going out."

Casey looked at her watch. "The Working Group goes on in a few minutes. We should go check it out."

Casey turned back to Dan. "This isn't over. If you did take Daisy, you'd better bring her back!"

SATURDAY AUGUST 2
1:47 P.M.

Casey and Mike sat in the stands and watched the Working Group get judged. Each dog went before the judge, one at a time. The judge examined the dog up close, and then asked the handler to walk the dog back and forth. After each dog had a turn, the judge often asked some of the dogs back into the ring for another look.

Casey knew the Working Group judge, a woman in a sparkly black dress named Margaret Bolligan. Judge Bolligan

32

seemed focused on two dogs in particular—Georgia Faller's Burmese Mountain Dog, Reggie, and Jason Temple's Newfoundland, Arthur.

"It looks like a close competition," Mike said.

"I don't want either one of them to win," Casey muttered.

Judge Bolligan walked around the ring one more time. As the crowd waited in suspenseful silence, she turned and pointed to her number one choice.

"The Burmese Mountain Dog," she said.

The crowd applauded. Georgia Faller jumped up and down. She pumped her fist in the air.

"Best in Show! Here we come!" she yelled. "Nothing can stop us!"

"Whoa. Pretty extreme," Mike remarked.

Jason Temple politely shook her hand. He waved to the crowd and led Arthur out of the ring.

"Come on," Casey said. "I want to talk to Jason."

Casey and Mike used their passes to get backstage.

33

Casey walked up to Jason.

"All right, Jason, you can give her back now," she said.

"What are you talking about?" Jason asked. Arthur panted patiently by his side.

"Daisy," Casey said. "I know you took her. You had Janet distract me. But since Arthur won't be in the Best of Show competition, you don't have to worry about Daisy beating him. So you can give her back."

"Casey Miller! What are you doing!"

Lisa ran up and stood between Casey and Jason.

"Jason, I'm sorry. Casey's very upset about Daisy getting loose. She's convinced somebody stole her. I'm sure she didn't mean to accuse you," Lisa said.

"But—" Casey protested.

"No buts," Lisa said. "You're coming with me."

Casey looked helplessly at Mike. Keep trying, she mouthed. Mike nodded.

Casey held back tears as Lisa led her away.

Dan Federman seemed like he was telling the truth. But could she trust him?

Jason was her strongest suspect, and she hadn't even had a chance to talk to him.

And then there was Georgia Faller. She was really competitive. She could have stolen Daisy to make sure Reggie won Best of Show.

But Lisa would never let her find out the truth now. And that meant only one thing.

She would never see Daisy again!

Under Lisa's watchful eye, Casey had spent the afternoon putting up flyers and calling local animal shelters. They walked for blocks all around the arena, but didn't find Daisy. They returned to the hotel, exhausted and defeated.

"Thanks for helping, Case," Lisa said, falling down on the bed. "I guess we've done all we can do."

"I guess so," Casey said, biting her lip. Having no hope left was the worst feeling in the world.

Someone knocked on the hotel room door.

"Who is it?" Lisa asked.

"It's Mike!"

Casey opened the door. Mike entered, holding a small tape recorder.

"I did what you said, Casey," Mike said in a low voice. "I kept trying. About an hour ago, Alex did a telephone interview with Jason Temple and Georgia Faller, to talk about the close decision today. I asked him to make a copy for me. I don't know if there's anything good on it. But I figure it's worth listening to."

Casey looked over at Lisa. Her sister shrugged.

"Just don't go around accusing people of stuff before you know for sure, okay?" she asked.

Casey's face flushed. "Okay."

Casey and Mike sat down at the small round table in the room. Mike pressed the PLAY button on the recorder. They listened to the tape.

"Oh well," Mike said, when it was over. "It was worth a try."

Casey looked at Mike, surprised. "Didn't you hear it?"

"Hear what?" Mike asked.

Casey grinned. "I know who took Daisy! The evidence is right there on the tape."

Can you solve the Case of the Disappearing Dog? Play Track 1 of the CD that came with your U-Solve-It! Mystery kit. Listen to the interviews carefully. See if you can figure out who stole Daisy. Then head over to the U-Solve-It! web site at **www.scholastic.com/usolveit** *to see if you're right.*

The Ghost of Wembley Manor

THURSDAY, JUNE 25
11:05 A.M.

"There it is! Wembley Manor."

George Ruiz stuck his head out of the window of the RV. The manor, a huge white house, sat on top of a small hill.

"That's supposed to be a haunted house?" George asked his father. It didn't look very scary.

Mr. Ruiz shrugged. "We won't know until we begin our investigation. That's why we're here."

The man driving the RV laughed. "Something tells me this case is a bust. Old Lady Wembley is like a hundred years old. She probably can't tell a ghost from a ham sandwich."

"That's not nice, Tony!" said a young woman in the back of the RV.

George still couldn't believe he was here, about to assist his father for the first time. George's dad was a paranormal investigator. Most people didn't know what that was.

"He's a ghost hunter," George would say, and then he usually got laughed at. He had to admit, "ghost hunter" didn't sound like a real job. George wasn't even sure if he believed in ghosts. But his dad took his job very seriously.

Mr. Ruiz traveled around to haunted houses. He and his team investigated them with scientific equipment. They tried to find out if a house was really haunted, or if there was a scientific explanation. Tony, the RV driver, was an expert on history and research. Shelley Carlson took all the photos and video footage of a haunted location. And Mr. Ruiz worked all of the other equipment.

George had always wanted to go on an investigation with his dad. Now that he was twelve and school was out, his dad had agreed to let him come. George couldn't wait to get inside the house. What would they find there? Objects flying through the air? Faces in the dark? He shivered just thinking about it.

The RV pulled up in front of the manor. The team

climbed out, and Mr. Ruiz looked them over. George knew his father liked the team to look as professional as possible.

"Most people do not take us seriously," Mr. Ruiz would always say. "That is why we must look serious."

To set an example for his team, Mr. Ruiz always neatly combed his dark hair and wore a white shirt and tie to every investigation. Shelley preferred jeans and a black T-shirt, but they were always clean, and she kept her light brown hair tied up in a ponytail. Tony, on the other hand, was the kind of guy who could never look professional. His shirts were always coming unbuttoned, his pants always seemed to be stained with ketchup or dirt, and there were always crumbs of food in his red beard.

George knew the only way to make his father happy was to dress exactly like him, so he had worn a white shirt and tie with his jeans. The shirt felt tight around the collar. He hoped Wembley Manor was air-conditioned.

"All right, team," Mr. Ruiz said. "Let's see what we've got here."

The team headed up the long walkway that led to the large front door. Before they even reached the door, it creaked open. In the shadows of the doorway, George saw a figure in white. The woman wore a white dress. Her white hair was piled on top of her head, and wrinkles creased her pale face.

George felt himself gasp a little. Was this a ghost?

"Welcome to Wembley Manor," she said, her voice trembling.

George relaxed. The woman had to be Winifred Wembley, the owner of the manor. George felt sheepish. He glanced at the others, hoping no one had seen his reaction.

Then a man appeared behind Mrs. Wembley. He looked to be about as old as George's dad, but he was almost a foot taller. He had short blond hair and wore a red plaid shirt and jeans. A huge ring of keys hung from his belt loop.

"I guess you're the ghost hunters," the man said, in a voice that showed he was clearly not impressed. "Well, boo! Ha ha."

George groaned silently. This guy seemed like a real jerk. He watched his father, who did not change his expression.

"Yes, we are Ruiz Paranormal Investigators," he said calmly. "May we come in?"

"Of course," Mrs. Wembley said in her tiny voice. Behind her, the man snorted.

"Whatever Aunt Winnie wants, Aunt Winnie gets," he said. "Come on in."

George followed the others into a large lobby. The floors were made of smooth marble, and a crystal chandelier hung overhead. George had never been in a rich person's house before, but he guessed this was what it must look like.

"Come into the sitting room, dears," Mrs. Wembley said. She walked slowly through a nearby doorway. The man in the plaid shirt rudely pushed past her, his keys jingling as he walked. Mr. Ruiz respectfully walked slowly behind Mrs. Wembley, and the rest of the team followed him.

Everything in the sitting room was a shade of white—creamy white walls, pearly white couches, and a white marble coffee table on top of a pale white rug. A man and a woman—about the same age as the man in plaid—sat on one of the couches. The woman had short blond hair. She wore a pink dress and pearls around her neck. She tapped her foot nervously on the wood floor. The man had messy, graying hair. He wore a green work shirt and tan pants. He

had a notepad in his hand and was busy scribbling away.

Mrs. Wembley took a seat in a high-backed chair with white cushions. She motioned for the rest of them to sit. George sat on one of the couches next to his dad. Tony and Shelley took a couch right next to them. The tall man stood in a corner, his arms folded.

Thank you for coming on such short notice," Mrs. Wembley began. "I should introduce myself. I am Winifred Wembley. And these are my niece and nephew, Bebe and Will."

She pointed to the man and woman on the couch. Then Mrs. Wembley pointed to the man in the corner. "And you've already met my other nephew, Warren."

Warren snorted. "Nephew? Don't you mean servant, Aunt Winnie?"

Bebe laughed nervously. "My brother's always joking. He's no servant. Aunt Winnie made him caretaker of the place. It's an important job."

Mr. Ruiz introduced the team members. Then he turned to face Mrs. Wembley. "Perhaps we should talk about why you have brought us here, Mrs. Wembley. You say this house is haunted?"

Mrs. Wembley nervously handled a white handkerchief in her hands. "I'm not sure. It started just a few weeks ago. Strange things happening at night. Sometimes I hear noises—

wails that just can't be human. And then there are those strange lights. And the messages—"

"Messages?" Mr. Ruiz asked, curious.

"A few times, words have appeared on my wall in glowing letters. But then they fade," Mrs. Wembley said.

"What kind of words?" Mr. Ruiz asked.

"They usually say the same thing," Mrs. Wembley said. She lowered her already weak voice to a whisper. "Get out!"

George felt a chill go through his body. He had heard about most of his father's cases. Strange noises and lights were very common. But ghostly messages—hardly ever. *Could this be the real thing?*

Mr. Ruiz looked around the room. "Has anyone else ever seen these messages?"

"Of course not," Warren said. "You can't see imaginary things!"

Bebe shyly raised her hand. "I haven't seen the messages," she said. "But I've heard—things."

"What about you, Will?" Mr. Ruiz asked.

Will Wembley was still writing in his notebook. His sister nudged him, and he looked up, startled.

"Oh, sorry," he said. "I'm working on calculations for my latest invention. No, I haven't seen or heard anything. Too busy working, I guess."

Mrs. Wembley looked at Mr. Ruiz with pleading in her

eyes. "Can you help us? I know something strange is going on."

Mr. Ruiz nodded. "I need to have a brief meeting with my team. We'll let you know our plan of action shortly."

Mrs. Wembley smiled gratefully. "Oh, thank you so much! I have a weak heart, you know. I don't think I can take much more of this."

"We'll do our best to help you," Mr. Ruiz assured her.

George hoped his dad was right. He wondered about those glowing messages. *How could a ghost make messages glow on a wall? And if it was a ghost doing it—how were they supposed to stop it?*

THURSDAY, JUNE 25
11:43 A.M.

The team held their meeting back in the RV. Tony turned on his laptop computer. Shelley started gathering her video equipment together while they talked.

"Looks like there's plenty of stuff we can try to tape here, between those lights and the glowing messages," she said. "I'll set up a feed wherever they've been reported. I can do night duty and keep watch on the monitors to see what the cameras pick up."

"Good idea," Mr. Ruiz said. "After you set up the feed, take a nap so you'll be ready for tonight. I'll do an EMF reading in every room of the house and see if there are any hot spots."

"What's EMF?" George asked.

"Electromagnetic frequency," Mr. Ruiz explained. "Just about everything gives off some kind of electric energy that can be measured with a detector. Humans, animals, refrigerators, TVs, power lines. The EMF detector blocks out big appliances and can read even very weak changes in electromagnetic fields. When ghosts are present, the field is disrupted, and you can chart it with the detector."

"I get it. So if you get unusual EMF readings in a place, that's a hot spot," George said. "Did you ever get a reading that was really caused by a ghost?"

"We have gotten readings that could indicate a ghost is present," Mr. Ruiz said. "But I've never seen a ghost myself. As a scientist, I look at the big picture. If there is enough other evidence, it *could* mean that a ghost is present."

"What other evidence?" George asked, but Tony interrupted them.

"You going to set up voice recorders, Al?"

Mr. Ruiz nodded. "Yes. I'd love to get a recording of those strange sounds. And who knows? We may get some EVP."

Now George felt confused. "EVP? Is that like EMFs?"

Mr. Ruiz shook his head. "No, that stands for Electronic Voice Phenomenon. That's when you set up a tape recorder in an empty room and record the sound there. There have been cases when the tape is played back and strange voices and messages are heard."

George shivered. "Pretty creepy."

"It's only creepy because it's unexplained," Mr. Ruiz said. "I believe that one day we will find a scientific explanation for all of these things."

"Hey, don't say that!" Tony said. "Then nobody will need us anymore."

"How about you, Tony?" Mr. Ruiz asked. "What have you found out about the Wembleys?"

"Well, we only got the call two days ago, so I haven't got much yet," he said, typing furiously on his keyboard. "Here's the basics. Mrs. Wembley's got a ton of money. She's outlived all of her relatives except for Bebe, Will, and Warren. Technically, she's their great aunt. She's got control of the family fortune, so the kids have all had to work for a living. Bebe used to be an actress. Will is some kind of inventor, but as far as I can tell, he's never invented anything that made money. And Warren used to be some big business guy, but the company went broke. That's why old lady Wembley made him the caretaker of the manor."

"So they're all broke, except for Mrs. Wembley," Shelley remarked.

"As far as I can tell, but I'll keep looking," Tony said.

"Well, it looks like we've got a plan," Mr. Ruiz said, standing up.

"What about me?" George asked. "What do I do?"

Mr. Ruiz smiled. "You can help me with the EMF readings."

George grinned. "All right!"

THURSDAY, JUNE 25
1:06 P.M.

After the team meeting, Mr. Ruiz explained the plan to the Wembley family. Mrs. Wembley and Bebe seemed relieved. Will seemed completely uninterested. And Warren seemed annoyed.

"You don't actually expect to sleep here, do you?" he asked.

"We will sleep in the RV," Mr. Ruiz said. "However, Shelley will need to set up a video center, so she can monitor the cameras we will be setting up. A small room in the house will do fine."

"The downstairs office might work," said Bebe.

"That would be great," Mr. Ruiz said, and George saw Warren Wembley frown.

Mrs. Wembley insisted that they eat lunch first. The meal was served at a long dining room table in another room with a chandelier. George munched on his ham sandwich and looked around the room, imagining ghosts swirling overhead. It just didn't seem possible. Haunted houses were supposed

to be dusty and creaky, not clean
and shiny.

After lunch, Tony and Shelley
went in different directions to
do their tasks. Mr. Ruiz took the
EMF detector from its case. It
looked like a black box the size of
a brick. On the face of it were
knobs and a gauge with a needle.

"What do we do?" George asked.

"We turn it on," Mr. Ruiz said. "And we walk around. I'll
let you know if I see any unusual readings."

Mr. Ruiz gave George a digital thermometer so he could
record the temperature in each room. If the temperature
jumped high or sank quickly, it could mean a ghost was
present, he explained.

They began in the basement, a clean space with a
laundry room and storage boxes. Then they worked their
way to the first floor. As they walked from room to room,
George realized Bebe was shadowing them. He didn't
notice her at first; she wore soft slippers on her small feet,
and they didn't make a sound on the floor.

"Well, hello, Miss Wembley," Mr. Ruiz said politely.

"I'm so curious to find out what's going on," Bebe said.
"I hope you don't mind."

"Of course not," Mr. Ruiz said.

George and his father continued his methodical sweep of every room. George was disappointed that the thermometer didn't change much, except for a few degrees now and then.

And he kept waiting for the EMF detector to beep, or give off smoke, or something, but nothing happened.

George did notice something unusual, though.

"Every room in this house is white," he remarked out loud. Except for the statues and paintings on the walls, the furniture, drapes, and paint in every room were in shades of white.

"Aunt Winnie is awfully fond of white," Bebe explained. "Every article of clothing she has is white. She's very particular."

More like peculiar, George thought to himself. *Maybe Tony was right. Maybe Mrs. Wembley is imagining everything.*

The only other interesting thing they saw during the sweep was Will Wembley's bedroom. It looked like a mad scientist's lab. The room was filled with tables and shelves of glass beakers, bottles of strange looking chemicals, tools, and pieces of metal in all kinds of weird shapes.

Mr. Ruiz did get some strange EMF readings in that room, but he thought they were probably from Will's equipment.

After what seemed like hours, Mr. Ruiz finished the EMF sweep in the attic.

"Did you find anything?" George asked.

Mr. Ruiz shook his head. "Nothing," he said. "But the paranormal events seem to be happening at night. Perhaps we'll find something then."

THURSDAY, JUNE 25
3:24 P.M.

After the EMF sweep, Mr. Ruiz checked in with Tony.

"Have you found out anything else?" he asked.

"Still working," Tony said. "So far, no strange deaths in the house, no abandoned burial grounds, anything like that. But here's something interesting. You know all those paintings and stuff in the house? They're worth a lot. Millions."

George whistled. "Imagine being that rich," he said.

"Money isn't everything," Mr. Ruiz said. "The Wembley family does not seem to be very happy."

"I guess you're right," George agreed.

Tony grinned. "And, I found one more thing. Check this out."

He grabbed a sheet of paper from the printer and handed it to Mr. Ruiz. George looked over his dad's arm to read it.

It was Bebe Wembley's acting resumé. There wasn't much on it. George wasn't sure what was supposed to be so interesting—until Mr. Ruiz put his finger on it.

"Hal's House of Horror, costumed performer," Mr. Ruiz read. He smiled.

"Isn't that the haunted house at the amusement park? Where people jump out at you?" George asked.

Mr. Ruiz nodded. "Interesting, don't you think? This is not the first time Bebe has been in a haunted house. In fact, she's been paid to scare people before. Good job, Tony."

"Hey, that's what I do," Tony replied.

"Why is that interesting?" George asked.

"I have never been the victim of a hoax before," Mr. Ruiz said. "Most people who call us sincerely believe their home is haunted. But messages on the wall—that's pretty rare. It's possible that someone in the house is trying to fool Mrs. Wembley into thinking there is a ghost here."

"But why would they want to do that?" George said, slightly disappointed. He was hoping, deep down, to see a real ghost.

"I don't know," Mr. Ruiz said. "But if someone is haunting the place, then it may very well be Bebe. She has the experience, after all."

"Yeah. And Bebe and Mrs. Wembley are the only ones who say they've heard or seen the ghost," Tony added.

George thought of what he knew about Bebe Wembley—small and quiet. He had a hard time imaging her scaring anybody. But she was an actress, after all.

Just then, George heard a sound outside the RV door—a jingling sound.

"Dad, I think someone's out there," he said.

Mr. Ruiz opened the door. Warren Wembley stood outside. It looked to George like he had been sneaking around, maybe listening at the door.

"Can I help you?" Mr. Ruiz asked.

Warren shook the keys on his belt. "I'm the caretaker, remember? I'm just taking care of things. Doing my job."

"Of course," Mr. Ruiz said.

THURSDAY, JUNE 25
4:00 P.M.

After meeting with Tony, Mr. Ruiz got the sound recording equipment ready.

"Mrs. Wembley and Bebe both reported hearing the sounds at night, after midnight," Mr. Ruiz explained. "I'm going to set up a recorder in each of their rooms. I'll time it so it won't start recording until eleven o'clock. The tape can record for six hours, so with luck we'll get something."

George helped his dad set up one recorder in Bebe's room, on her dresser. When they got to Mrs. Wembley's room, they noticed there wasn't much furniture in the room. Mrs. Wembley's nightstand was covered with several bottles of medicine. Folded laundry sat on top of her dresser.

"Let's put it under the bed," George suggested. "That way Mrs. Wembley won't trip over it if she gets up during the night."

"Good idea, George," Mr. Ruiz said. "I knew bringing you along would be a good thing."

George smiled, happy with his dad's praise. He was having fun so far. Maybe one day, when he was old enough, he could join the team for real.

After setting up the voice recorders, Mr. Ruiz checked in with Shelley in the office on the first floor. She had completely taken it over. George was amazed to see several monitors set up. Each one showed a major room in Wembley Manor: the dining room, sitting room, and of course, Mrs. Wembley's bedroom, where the hauntings were supposed to have happened. Will and Warren had apparently asked that their rooms not be filmed.

"It's not such a big deal, because they haven't experienced any hauntings, anyway," Shelley said. "It all seems to center around Mrs. Wembley. If anything happens, I'll see it, Al."

"Excellent!" said Mr. Ruiz. "It looks like we're going to be

ready for whatever happens tonight."

Suddenly, one of the screens flickered, and the picture went out. Shelley frowned.

"That's the feed from Mrs. Wembley's room," she said. "Hey George, you want to go upstairs and check the cord on the camera for me? See if it's loose? You know where to go, right?"

"Sure," George said, feeling important. It was nice that Shelley trusted him to help.

George walked to the main staircase and up the stairs. He was about to turn down the hallway when he heard two loud voices coming from a nearby room.

"Just help me talk some sense into her, Will." It was Warren Wembley. "I've got to have that money by Saturday, or I'm in big trouble."

"That's your problem, Warren," Will said. "I've asked Aunt Winnie for money to fund my inventions, and she always says no. Why do you think she'll help you?"

"She just has to sell one of these stupid paintings, and all our troubles would be over," Warren grumbled.

"I know," Will said. "Believe me, I'd do anything to get some cash from Aunt Winnie. But it's not going to happen. Not until she leaves this house, so we can sell some of this stuff. Or until . . ." His voice trailed off.

"Don't get your hopes up. She'll probably live to be two hundred," Warren said.

George suddenly realized he was eavesdropping. He hurried down the hallway, but bumped into Warren, who was stepping out of a doorway.

"Can I *help* you?" Warren asked.

George blushed. "Just heading to Mrs. Wembley's room."

Warren pointed down the hallway. "On the right."

George nodded in thanks and hurried to the bedroom. He found the camera. Just as Shelley had guessed, the cord connection was loose. He tightened it and then headed back downstairs.

As he walked, the conversation between Warren and Will preyed on his mind. The way the two brothers had talked about their aunt's money was kind of creepy.

Creepier than a ghost, even, George thought.

George went back to the office. Shelley was smiling happily.

"Thanks, George," she said. "You fixed it."

"Yeah," George answered absently. He wasn't sure if he should talk about what he had heard. But he was supposed to be helping the investigation. And he had a feeling that this might help.

"Dad, I just heard something upstairs," George began.

"Something ghostly?" Mr. Ruiz asked.

"Not exactly," George said. He described the strange conversation between Warren and Will Wembley.

Mr. Ruiz looked thoughtful. "Hmm. This could provide a motive."

"A motive for what?" Shelley asked, curious.

"Dad thinks maybe someone in the house is causing the hauntings," George explained.

Shelley raised an eyebrow. "Really?"

"I'm not sure. Those ghostly messages are suspicious," George's dad answered. "And now it seems that Mrs. Wembley's nephews would like her to leave the house, so they can sell her art. Perhaps . . ."

"They're trying to scare her out!" George finished. *That made sense. With Mrs. Wembley out of the way, they could sell the art and keep the money.*

"Not bad thinking," Shelley said. "But how the heck are we going to prove that?"

Mr. Ruiz waved his arm around the room. "Whatever happens tonight, we'll see it."

George shivered with anticipation. Whether the ghost was real or not, this was turning out to be an exciting case. And now the video and voice recorders were all set up. *Who knew what they might find?*

THURSDAY, JUNE 25
11:01 P.M.

That evening Mr. Ruiz had taken the team out to a local diner for supper. By the time they had finished eating, the sun was starting to set. George felt a quiver of excitement as they drove back to the manor. When they walked back inside, they were greeted by Bebe.

"Aunt Winnie has already gone to bed," she explained. "She's very tired these days. I'll be up for a while, though. May I watch you work?"

"I'll be doing some more EMF readings, but you've already seen that," Mr. Ruiz said. "Why don't you watch the video monitors with Shelley?"

"Oh, that would be lovely," Bebe said.

George tapped his dad's arm. "Can I talk to you for a second?"

Mr. Ruiz turned to Bebe. "Excuse me." He and George walked back outside.

"Is it a good idea to let Bebe watch what we're doing?" George asked. "What if she's the one causing the hauntings?"

"Then we will be able to keep an eye on her," Mr. Ruiz answered. "We have nothing to hide. There is no harm in letting Bebe watch. Although, I might feel better if you stayed in the video room, too."

George felt a surge of pride knowing that his dad wanted him to help keep watch.

"Thanks!" he said.

"I'll come get you when it's time to go back to the RV," Mr. Ruiz told him. "Now, let's go back inside."

So for the next few hours George sat with Bebe and Shelley in the office, watching the cameras. George kept waiting to see something in one of the rooms—a shadow, a floating figure, moving furniture, anything—but everything was calm and quiet. It would have been boring, George realized, except that Bebe was asking Shelley a lot of questions about ghost hunting. Shelley had some great stories to tell.

After a few hours, Mr. Ruiz walked in.

"I think we're going to hit the sack, George," he said. "Shelley's got everything covered here."

"Okay," George said, standing up. He yawned and stretched.

"I guess I'll get some sleep, too," Bebe said. She looked at

George's dad. "I'm not sure if Aunt Winnie is really seeing things or not, Mr. Ruiz. But I do hope you find something that will put her mind at rest. I worry about her."

"We'll do our best, Miss Wembley," Mr. Ruiz assured her.

As Bebe stood up, something slipped from her pocket onto the floor. It looked like a business card. George picked it up and handed it to her. He quickly glanced at the name.

LANCE WENTWORTH
Dealer in Fine Art

"Thank you," Bebe said. She quickly put the card in her pocket.

Dealer in Fine Art, George thought. He couldn't help remembering what Tony had said about the paintings in the manor—worth millions. Mrs. Wembley wasn't interested in selling them. *So what was Bebe doing with that card?*

"George, let's go," his dad said.

As George and his dad walked back to the RV, George told his father about the business card.

"Do you think she's trying to sell Mrs. Wembley's paintings?" George asked. "Maybe she wants to get money from them, just like her brothers were saying."

"I don't know," Mr. Ruiz said. "One business card is not enough evidence to prove that. But I agree that it is suspicious."

When they got back to the RV, they found Tony already snoring away on one of the beds. George and his dad changed into sweats.

"Just in case something happens during the night," Mr. Ruiz said. "We don't want to get caught in our pajamas."

"You think of everything, huh, Dad?" George remarked, climbing into a sleeping bag on one of the pullout beds.

"I try," Mr. Ruiz replied.

Then George fell into a deep sleep.

FRIDAY, JUNE 26
2:58 A.M.

"Al! Tony! Wake up! We've got a problem!"

George groggily woke from his sleep. His dad and Tony were already out of bed. Shelley's voice streamed through the intercom in the RV.

"What's going on, Shelley?" Mr. Ruiz asked.

"I lost the video feed. All of it. Everything's black."

George shivered. *Was something happening? Something ghostly?*

"We'll be right there," Mr. Ruiz said. He began to slip on his sneakers.

"Can I come, too?" George asked.

"Of course," his dad replied.

George, Mr. Ruiz, and Tony hurried up the walkway to the manor. Shelley opened the door for them.

"It's weird," she said. "All of the cameras went out at once. That's never happened before."

Suddenly, a loud scream came from upstairs. Mr. Ruiz raced toward the sound, and the others followed him. They stopped in front of Mrs. Wembley's room. The door was wide open.

Mr. Ruiz stepped inside, and George was surprised to see Bebe rush up to him, wearing red silk pajamas. But he couldn't see past his father into the room to see anything else.

"It's Aunt Winnie!" Bebe wailed. "She's dead!"

> **FRIDAY, JUNE 26**
> **3:26 A.M.**

The next few hours seemed like a blur to George, like some kind of nightmare. Mr. Ruiz calmed down Bebe and quickly called for an ambulance. Will Wembley came out of his room wearing a red bathrobe, his gray hair tousled. Warren Wembley came in from outside, his keys jangling on his belt.

"I was just out checking the grounds, like I do every night," he said. "What happened?"

Mr. Ruiz took Warren aside and quietly explained what had happened. Warren looked shocked.

"Surely . . . she can't be . . . "

Bebe came out of the room, tears streaming from her cheeks.

"They can't revive her," she said. "She's had a heart attack."

She threw herself into her brother Will's arms and began to sob.

Mr. Ruiz nodded to the team, and they quietly headed downstairs.

"Let's gather up our equipment as quickly as we can," he said. "George, help Shelley with the video cameras."

George nodded and followed Shelley to the office.

"I can't believe she's dead," George said. "That's really sad. I mean, we just saw her."

"I know," Shelley said. "I feel really bad."

Shelley paused in front of the office door. "Hey, what's this?"

She picked up the thick black cord that connected the monitors to the video camera feeds. The cord had been sliced cleanly through.

"I guess we're not dealing with a ghost here," she said, frowning. "I've never heard of a ghost cutting wires before."

"Or a ghost with footprints," George said. "Look."

Right next to the cut wire was a pair of muddy footprints. George saw that they extended down the hall to one of the mansion's side doors.

"Very interesting," Shelley said. She unclipped a camera from her belt and snapped a picture.

"If that's a ghost, he's got big feet," Shelley remarked.

"Did you see anything strange on the video feed before the line got cut?" George asked.

"No," Shelley said. Then she looked thoughtful. "As a matter of fact, I did. Will Wembley was pacing up and down the hallways for about an hour. Then he left for a while, and came back. I thought he was just thinking—you know, inventor stuff. But he did seem awfully nervous."

Now it was George's turn to be thoughtful. "Hmm. I wonder why somebody would want to cut the video feed on purpose?" he asked.

"Maybe somebody didn't want us to see something," Shelley said, her eyes looking upstairs. "Something bad."

George shivered. He thought he knew what Shelley was trying to say.

Had Mrs. Wembley been murdered?

FRIDAY, JUNE 26
4:57 A.M.

The ghost hunting team had all their equipment packed and stacked by the front door, ready to leave. But George was hesitant to go.

"Something doesn't feel right," he told his dad. "The footprints prove that the video feed was cut on purpose. We already thought somebody was scaring Mrs. Wembley on purpose. Maybe they wanted more than that. Maybe they wanted her . . . dead."

"But Mrs. Wembley died of a heart attack," Tony pointed out. "She had a weak heart, remember?"

Shelley's eyes widened. "That's right. Everybody knew that. And everybody knows what a good scare can do to somebody with a weak heart."

George realized Shelley was right. "That's it! Somebody tried to give her a heart attack. That has to be what happened! We can't go now, Dad. We have to prove it!"

Mr. Ruiz frowned. "We are not the police, George. We are ghost hunters. Perhaps I will tell the police what has happened here. But right now, we must leave. We'll come back after things have calmed down and get the equipment out of Mrs. Wembley's room."

But then Bebe Wembley came down the stairs, still in her pajamas.

"Please don't go yet," she said. "I need to talk to you."

"Of course," Mr. Ruiz said.

"I think there's something more to my aunt's heart attack," Bebe began. "I woke up because I heard a noise—a ghostly noise. It was coming from Aunt Winnie's room. When I went to check on her, she wasn't . . . "

"I know," Mr. Ruiz said. "I am so sorry."

"I think a ghost frightened my aunt to death," Bebe said.

George studied Bebe. *Did she really believe a ghost had scared her aunt? She seemed completely sincere. But then again,* he reminded himself, *she was an actress.*

"I want you to help me prove it," Bebe continued. "Did you see anything on the video camera?"

"Nope," Shelley said. "Somebody cut the wire to the feed."

Bebe looked surprised. "You mean on purpose?"

Shelley shrugged. "I don't know."

"Well, that just proves that something strange is going on," Bebe said. "Please, please do this for me. Just take a look at my aunt's room."

Mr. Ruiz looked at George. "This is more than I expected, George. You can go back to the RV if you want."

George shook his head. "No. I think something strange did happen to Mrs. Wembley. And I want to find out what it is."

Mr. Ruiz nodded. "All right, then. Let's go."

They followed Bebe back to Mrs. Wembley's room. Morning sunlight streamed through the windows. Her bed was now empty. The medicine bottles and piles of laundry were still there, just as George had remembered from the day before.

Shelley walked around the room, snapping photos. Mr. Ruiz took some EMF readings. George wasn't hopeful.

The room looked bright and very clean. *What ghostly evidence would they find?*

Then George spotted something out of place—something on one of the window's white curtains.

"Dad, look," George said. "A red thread."

Mr. Ruiz carefully picked it up. "Not exactly ghostly," he said.

"But it is strange," George pointed out. "Mrs. Wembley only had white clothes, remember?"

Mr. Ruiz raised an eyebrow. "Good observation, George."

But George frowned, remembering the previous night. "It doesn't help much. Bebe is wearing red pajamas. Will Wembley wore a red bathrobe. And Warren had on a red plaid shirt. Any one of them could have been in this room last night and left the thread."

Then George's discovery was overshadowed by an exclamation from Shelley.

"Hey! Get a load of this!" she called out.

Shelley had closed the wide open door to check behind it. At the top of the door, in glowing letters, was a ghostly message: GET OUT!

Shelley snapped a photo of the message.

"So there really is a ghost!" Bebe gasped.

"Perhaps," Mr. Ruiz said. "But I have another idea. Tony, please bring me a sample kit."

Tony nodded and ran downstairs. He came back a minute later with a plastic jar in a sealed bag, along with a small plastic scraper. Mr. Ruiz took the kit and removed the plastic jar. He opened it and then gently scraped some of the glowing message into the bag. George noticed his father had to stand on his tiptoes to reach the glowing words.

Must have been a really tall ghost, George mused. The large footprints came to mind.

"This could be ghostly," Mr. Ruiz said. "But I suspect not. Before I became a paranormal investigator, I worked for the power company. This looks like the chemical found in industrial road flares. It glows brightly for a short time, but fades in a few hours."

George immediately thought of the chemicals in Will Wembley's room. And his strange pacing before the video feed was cut. *Could Will have cut the video feed and then left the glowing message on the door?*

George's father turned to Bebe. "I can have this analyzed, of course. But right now the evidence points to something other than a ghost. The cut video feed. The footprints. The message. Even the red thread George found. They all point to a human rather than something paranormal."

"What exactly are you saying?" Bebe asked.

"Just that I think someone might have been scaring your aunt on purpose," Mr. Ruiz said.

Bebe looked stunned. "Why would someone do something so cruel?"

"I don't know," Mr. Ruiz said. "Perhaps this is a matter for the police."

Bebe sank to the bed. "The police? Oh no. What that would do to the Wembley name . . ."

Mr. Ruiz looked at the team. "I think we've done all we can here."

Bebe stood up. "Of course. And thank you. Thank you for trying to help."

George was about to turn toward the door when he suddenly remembered something.

"Dad! Wait! The voice recorder!" he said.

Mr. Ruiz slapped his forehead. "How could I forget?"

George walked to the bed and took the voice recorder out from under it. The machine had already stopped recording.

"Miss Wembley, I think we should listen to this," Mr. Ruiz said.

Bebe nodded. "Definitely. Let's go to the sitting room."

The team followed Bebe downstairs. George carried the recorder and placed it on the coffee table in the center of the room. His father excused himself to get some equipment from the truck. When he returned, he took a seat in front of the recorder.

George sat next to his father. He was eager to hear the tape. He hadn't had a chance to talk to anyone on the way downstairs, but he had a few ideas.

Whoever had scared Mrs. Wembley had probably been wearing red. That could be Bebe, Will, and Warren. They all had motives to want Mrs. Wembley out of the house. Will and Warren had talked about selling Mrs. Wembley's valuable art. And Bebe had a business card from an art dealer.

But whoever had cut the video feed had big feet. He knew that from the footprints. And they had probably been tall, because they had written the message high on the door. That ruled out Bebe.

So who was guilty, Will or Warren? Will had been seen pacing the halls last night, and then vanished for awhile. He also had chemicals in his room that could have left the ghostly message.

Warren needed money, fast. And he had been hanging around the trailer that first day, maybe spying on them.

Mystery #1
Mystery #2
Mystery #3

But as his father liked to say, that wasn't enough evidence. They needed more.

George hoped the tape would hold the answers.

Will and Warren Wembley entered the sitting room.

"What's this about a voice tape?" Warren asked.

"Yesterday, George and I placed a voice recorder under Mrs. Wembley's bed," Mr. Ruiz explained. "It was set on a timer, and recorded everything from eleven o'clock until five o'clock this morning."

Warren frowned. "I didn't know about that."

"It's standard in a haunting investigation," Mr. Ruiz said. "Now, according to my notes, Shelley's video feed was cut at approximately two fifty-five in the morning. We heard Bebe's scream a few moments later. So I'm going to rewind the tape back to that time."

Mr. Ruiz pressed a button on the recorder. The sitting room was quiet except for the whirring of the tape. He played the tape. George listened carefully. There was a ghostly wail, some muffled sounds, and a few moments later, the sound of Bebe's scream.

"Well, that doesn't prove anything," Warren said, folding his arms across his chest.

"Play it again," George said. "I think I heard something."

Mr. Ruiz raised an eyebrow, but he rewound the tape without a word. He played the section again.

George stood up, excited. "I know who the ghost is," he said. "The evidence is right there on the tape!"

Do you know the identity of the Ghost of Wembley Manor? Play Track 2 of the CD that came with your U-Solve-It! *Mystery kit. Listen to the recording carefully. See if you can figure out who the ghost is. Then check the* U-Solve-It! *web site to see if you're right!*

The Case of the Super-Fried Hard Drive

TUESDAY, MARCH 14
8:45 A.M.

"**T**hanks for bringing me to Take Your Kid to Work Day," Matt Gilardi told his uncle Ralph.

Uncle Ralph looked in the rearview mirror and scowled at Matt, who sat in the backseat of Ralph's sports car.

"You're not my kid," Ralph said. "I'm just doing this as a favor to your mom."

Matt just shrugged and took a bite of his cereal bar. He was used to his uncle's grumpy moods. Ralph was his mom's younger brother. When Matt was little, Uncle Ralph was always too busy playing video games to play with him. Now that Uncle Ralph was a video game designer, he was still too busy working to ever spend time with Matt.

Matt didn't mind so much. Uncle Ralph wasn't that much fun, anyway. But when Take Your Kid to Work Day came around, Matt had begged his mom to ask Ralph to take him. How cool would it be to spend the day at a video game company?

Matt's knee bounced up and down in anticipation. He took another bite of his cereal bar.

"Hey! Don't get any crumbs in my car!" Ralph barked.

"Sorry," Matt said. He brushed some crumbs off of his jeans, then realized that's exactly what Ralph *didn't* want him to do.

Thankfully, Ralph steered the car into a parking lot just then. Matt looked out the window to see a five-story office building with big glass windows. Palm trees lined the path to the building's front door.

Ralph pulled into a parking space right near the path.

"Sweet space!" Matt remarked.

"That's one of the perks of being a top designer," Ralph said. "Your mom always said I was wasting my time playing video games all those years. But that's what got me where I am today."

Ralph and Matt stepped out of the car and into the bright California sunshine.

"Just try and be cool today, okay?" Ralph asked. "Don't go bugging anybody or breaking anything."

"Right, like I'm three years old or something," Matt said. "Give me a break."

Ralph sighed and headed into the building. Matt followed. They took the elevator to the fifth floor. A young woman with brown, curly hair sat behind a big desk. On the wall behind the desk was the company's logo: XTreme Video.

"Hi, Ralph," the woman said. Then she smiled. "Hey, is this your nephew?"

"Yeah, this is Matt," Ralph said. "Matt, this is Marla, the receptionist."

"Hi," Matt said.

"How old are you?" Marla asked.

"Eleven," Matt answered.

Marla looked from Ralph to Matt. "Wow, you two look exactly alike," she said. "Did anyone ever tell you that?"

Ralph scowled. Matt looked up at his uncle, slightly alarmed. He wasn't sure he wanted to be like his uncle in any way. But Marla was right. They both had brown wavy hair and brown eyes. They were definitely dressed differently, though. Matt's mom had made him wear a shirt with a collar and nice pants. Ralph wore a T-shirt that said I HATE EVERYTHING, jeans torn at the knee, and scruffy sneakers.

"Your nephew dresses better than you, though,"

Marla remarked, as though she had read Matt's mind.

Ralph just frowned. "Come on, Matt. Let's go to my office."

Matt followed his uncle down a hallway. Matt stopped when he stepped inside the office, staring. The walls were covered with posters of Ralph's video games, Robot Fighter 1 and 2. Action figures of the video game characters crowded Ralph's desk.

"Wow!" Matt cried. He walked over to the desk. But before he could grab a figure, Ralph grabbed his hand.

"No touching!" Ralph scolded. "Those are collectors' items."

There was a knock on the door, and another young woman stepped inside. Her long, dark hair flowed down her back. She wore a long, black skirt with silver buttons down the front, cowboy boots, and a purple tank top.

"Nice T-shirt," the woman said. "You're setting a great example for your nephew."

"Matt, this is my assistant, Rachel," Ralph said.

"Hi," Matt said. "Nice to meet you."

Rachel smiled. "Wow, you're polite. Are you sure you're Ralph's nephew?"

"Very funny," Ralph said. "What do you want?"

"Just reminding you there's a meeting with the boss at eleven," Rachel told him. "He wants some details on the new game."

Ralph sighed. "How many times do I have to tell him. . . You can't rush genius!"

"Well, you can tell him again at eleven," Rachel said.

Rachel left, and Ralph sat down at his computer. He started checking his e-mail.

"Uncle Ralph, are you really working on a new game?" Matt asked.

Ralph lowered his voice. "It's top secret. I haven't even told anyone what it's about yet. But when this game comes out, it's going to change the world of video games. It's that awesome."

Matt was impressed. His uncle might be kind of a jerk, but he was really smart.

Ralph turned back to his computer, completely ignoring Matt.

Matt tapped his uncle on the shoulder. "Hey, Uncle Ralph? Aren't you supposed to show me around or something?"

Ralph looked up from the computer screen. "Yeah, right," he said. He picked up the telephone and pushed a button. "Hey, Rachel. Get back here and show my nephew around."

TUESDAY, MARCH 14
9:30 A.M.

At first Matt was a little hurt that Ralph didn't want to show him around, but he quickly realized he'd have more fun with Rachel.

"So I guess you like video games, Matt?" Rachel asked, as they walked down a hallway.

Matt nodded. "A lot."

"Me, too," Rachel said. "I always knew I wanted to be a game designer when I grew up."

"You're a designer?" Matt asked.

"Designer in training," Rachel said. "I just got out of college. I'm supposed to be learning the ropes from Ralph, helping him with his new game. But he won't let me do much except order his pizza."

Matt noticed that Rachel lost the friendly tone in her voice when she talked about his uncle Ralph. He didn't blame her. It didn't sound like his uncle was treating her all that fairly.

"Ever play Alien Planet?" Rachel asked him.

"Of course!" Matt cried. "That is probably the sweetest game in the world. Next to my uncle's games, I mean."

Rachel grinned. "Well, then check this out."

Matt followed Rachel into an office. Posters for the video game Alien Planet covered the walls. Planets hung on strings from the ceiling. There was a huge, round desk in the center of the room. A man with dark hair sat behind it, munching on something in a small bag. He smiled when he saw Rachel.

"Kenji, this is Matt," Rachel said. "He's here for Take Your Kid to Work Day."

"Cool," the man said.

"Matt, this is Kenji Nekoi, the creator of Alien Planet."

"Man, that is so cool!" Matt said. "I love that game. My favorite is that underground level, where you fight the alien with twelve heads. It took me forever to figure out how to defeat it."

"Thanks," Kenji said. He stood up and held the bag out to Matt. "Want some?"

"Sure," Matt replied. He never turned down a snack. He stuck his hand in the bag and pulled out what looked like a green pea. Strange—but still a snack. He popped it in his mouth.

"Hey!" Matt cried. The little pea burned with spicy heat.

"I should have warned you," Rachel said. "Wasabi peas. They're a hot Japanese snack. Kenji's favorite."

"They keep my brain focused," Kenji said.

"Yeah, I can see that," Matt replied.

"Now that Kenji's done torturing you, I'll show you some other stuff," Rachel said.

Matt tried to remember everything Rachel showed him, because he knew he'd have to write a report about it in school the next day. He met the people who sold the games in stores and the people who made ads and TV commercials about the games. But his favorite room was the Testing Room.

Three guys sat behind three large computer monitors, playing video games. Rachel introduced them: Sal, who was short and kind of chubby; Pete, who was medium height with red hair; and Greg, who was really tall and thin.

"And this is Matt," Rachel explained to the men. "He's here for Take Your Kid to Work Day. He wants to know about what you do."

"That's easy," Sal said, his eyes on the game. "We play video games all day. And we get paid!"

"No way," Matt said. "For real?"

Pete nodded. "We test the games before they go into stores. Make sure there are no glitches or anything."

"That sounds like a dream job," Matt said.

"More like a nightmare sometimes," Pete grumbled. "Imagine doing the same thing over and over like, five thousand times . . ."

Sal blasted a zombie coming toward him on the computer screen. "Don't bring the boy down, Pete! This job is a total blast."

"Speak for yourself," said Greg, pausing his game. "I want to design my own games, not just test them. I had a great idea for one, but Robot Ralph told the boss not to do it. He said it was childish and stupid. What a jerk that guy is."

Matt frowned. *Yeah, Ralph* was *a jerk sometimes. But he was still family!*

"Hey, Greg, cool it," Rachel said. "Matt is Ralph's nephew."

"Well, thanks for warning me," Greg said. "Sorry, kid."

"It's okay," Matt replied.

Rachel looked at her watch. "I've got some stuff to do. Let's go see your uncle."

TUESDAY, MARCH 14
10:55 A.M.

Matt returned to Ralph's office just as his uncle was leaving for his meeting.

"Stay here while I'm gone," Ralph said. "Don't touch anything, okay?"

"Okay," Matt said. "I can work on my report."

"Don't touch the computer," Ralph said. "I mean it, Matt!"

"Okay, okay!" Matt said. "Chill out."

Ralph left, and Matt sat on a purple couch facing his uncle's desk. Matt looked around at the posters on the walls, but he quickly grew bored. Then his stomach started to rumble.

Who knew how long Ralph would be in that meeting? Matt wondered. *It wasn't fair. There was probably a snack machine or something in the building. He could grab something and be back before Ralph knew he was gone.*

Matt walked back to the lobby desk.

"Hey, is there a snack machine around here somewhere?" Matt asked Marla.

"Down the hall, third door on the right," Marla told him. "It's the break room."

Matt followed Marla's directions into a room with a black-and-white floor and black metal tables. Four snack machines lined the back wall.

"Perfect!" Matt said. He dug in his pockets for change. Soon he was sitting at one of the black tables, munching on peanut butter crackers and a soda.

From where he sat, Matt could see through a side doorway in the game room. It looked like there was a video game machine in there. Curious, Matt ate his last cracker and walked through the door.

"Now, that's *really* sweet!" Matt exclaimed. The tiny room was crammed with video game machines, like an arcade. Matt realized they were all games put out by XTreme Video. He walked up to Alien Planet 3 and pushed the start button. The screen lit up.

"No quarters," Matt said. *That meant he could play and play.* . . .

Matt started playing the game. He was a cyborg warrior, sent to an alien planet to destroy all hostile life forms there. He loaded up his laser blaster and ran through the alien jungle. . . .

He wasn't sure how much time had passed when Marla came to the doorway.

"Hey, Matt, I think your uncle's looking for you," she said. "He's like, yelling really loud."

"Oh, thanks," Matt said. He turned off the game. His uncle was probably pretty mad.

But Matt wasn't prepared for how upset Uncle Ralph really was. When he walked into the office, Ralph was stomping back and forth, screaming.

"I told you not to touch my computer!" he yelled. "I told you!"

"But I didn't," Matt protested.

"Yeah, right," Ralph said. "I know you did. My hard drive is fried. Totally fried! My work is lost, and it's all your fault!"

> **TUESDAY, MARCH 14**
> **12:10 P.M.**

Rachel ran in. "What's the problem?" she asked Ralph.

"My computer's crashed. Totally wiped out," he replied. "Matt was messing around with it."

"Was not!" Matt cried.

Rachel shook her head. "Chill out," she told him. "I back up your hard drive every night, remember? The disks are in here."

Rachel walked to the desk and opened a drawer. She looked confused. "That's weird," she said. "The backups aren't here."

She frantically began opening the other desk drawers. "I can't find them. Do you think somebody stole them?"

"I bet they did!" Matt said. "See, that proves I didn't mess with your computer. Why would I steal your disks, too?"

"Because—I—I don't know!" Ralph sputtered. "I just know everything was fine until I brought you here."

He ran his hands through his hair, then sank down on his desk chair. The chair was low to the ground, and Ralph missed the mark and tumbled to the floor. He let out an angry cry.

"See, that proves it!" Ralph cried, standing up again. "You were messing around with my chair, too!"

"It wasn't me!" Matt yelled.

Ralph walked to the door. "I already called your mom," he told Matt. "But she can't leave work early to pick you up. So I'm stuck with you."

"Maybe *I'm* stuck with *you*," Matt muttered, his feelings hurt.

"Whatever. I'm going for a walk. Just stay out of trouble." Then Ralph disappeared down the hallway.

Rachel put an arm around Matt's shoulder. "Don't take it personally. Your uncle's been working really hard on that game concept. It's like his baby. He'll calm down soon."

"I guess," Matt said.

"Listen, I've got some work to do," Rachel said. "Are you okay? What are you going to do?"

"I don't know," Matt said, but he was lying. He knew exactly what he was going to do.

Before the day was over, he was going to find out who fried his uncle's hard drive and stole his disks.

Now, what's the first thing a detective does when he investigates a crime? Matt asked himself. His mom loved to watch those crime shows on TV. He had to remember something about them. . . .

"Of course! Examine the scene of the crime," Matt said out loud. That would be Ralph's office.

Matt looked around. The desk would be the obvious place to start. He walked over to it. TV detectives always dusted for fingerprints. But Matt had no idea how to do that. So he looked around.

The desk looked the same as before—a mess of action figures. Matt sighed. He wasn't even sure what he was supposed to be looking for.

Then something shiny caught his eye, right next to the keyboard. Matt picked it up. It was a shiny silver button.

Could it be a clue? Matt wasn't sure. But he slipped it into his pocket.

Matt looked some more, but didn't see anything else unusual.

I'm doing this all wrong, he told himself. *I should be talking to people. I need to find out who would want to ruin Uncle Ralph's game.*

Matt started to walk to the door. Then he felt something

crunch underneath his sneaker. He looked under his foot to see a pile of tiny green crumbs.

He bent down. Among the crumbs was what looked like a tiny, green pea. He picked it up and sniffed it.

"Wasabi pea," he said. "Kenji's favorite snack."

But Kenji had seemed so nice. Would he really have fried Uncle Ralph's hard drive?

There was only one way to find out.

```
TUESDAY, MARCH 14
12:56 P.M.
```

Matt walked up to the reception desk.

"Hi, Marla," he said.

"Hey," she replied. "I heard about what happened to your uncle. That stinks."

"Yeah it does, especially because he thinks I did it," Matt said.

Marla shook her head. "That's not fair," she muttered. "I hate to break this to you, kid, but there are plenty of people here who don't like your uncle. Any one of them could have done it."

"Like who?" Matt asked.

"Like everybody," Marla said. "He's either insulted or yelled at just about everyone in the office. He's a hot head, that guy."

"Yeah, I know," Matt admitted. "So even Kenji Nekoi doesn't like him?"

"Especially Kenji Nekoi," Marla said. "Kenji wanted to use the band Slime Doggies to create the music for Alien Planet 3. But Ralph got them for Robot Fighters 2, even though he knew Kenji wanted them. Boy, Kenji really freaked out."

Matt understood. Slime Doggies were one of the hottest bands around, and everyone knew great music could really make a video game popular.

"So, Marla, I was wondering. Do you have a tape recorder I could borrow?" Matt asked.

"Sure," Marla replied, opening a drawer in her desk. "I use it to record meetings sometimes. What do you need it for?"

"For my, uh, school report," Matt lied. "I need to interview people about my day here at the office, and I forgot to bring a tape recorder."

Marla handed it to him. "There's a fresh tape in there. Knock yourself out."

"Thanks," Matt said. He tucked the tape recorder under his arm.

He knew exactly who he wanted to speak to first.

"So Kenji, thanks for letting me interview you," Matt said. He sat in a chair on the other side of Kenji's desk. Kenji sat in front of his computer, pouring hot sauce from a bottle onto a burrito. He took a big bite.

"Want some?" he asked Matt.

"No, thanks," Matt replied, remembering the burn from that wasabi pea. "I just want to ask you some questions about your job. For my school report."

"Sure," Kenji said.

"So, how did you become a video game designer?" Matt asked.

"Well, it all started when I was twelve . . ." Kenji began.

Twenty minutes later, Matt had heard Kenji's whole life story. But he had no idea if Kenji had fried his uncle's hard drive or not. Matt thought of the wasabi pea on the floor. He tried a different question.

"Hey, did you go into my uncle's office today, by any chance?" he asked.

Kenji thought. "Oh yeah. I went to ask him if he wanted me to order him a burrito. But nobody was there."

Matt stood up. "Thanks, Kenji," he said. But before he turned off the tape, he had an idea.

"I played Alien Planet 3 today," Matt said. "Good music."

"Yeah," Kenji agreed. "I wanted to use Slime Doggies. But I got The Fangs instead. I thought it turned out much better."

"The music is awesome," Matt said. He turned off the recorder. "Thanks!"

"No problem," Kenji said. Then he took another bite of burrito.

TUESDAY, MARCH 14
2:00 P.M.

Matt walked down the hall, feeling a little bummed out. He was so sure Kenji had sabotaged his uncle. But he hadn't been able to prove anything.

As Matt walked past the game tester's room, he saw the tall figure of Greg hunched over his computer. Matt remembered Greg's complaint about his uncle. *What a jerk that guy is*, Greg had said.

It's worth a try, Matt thought. He walked up to Greg.

"Hey," he said. "Can I interview you for my school report?"

Greg raised an eyebrow. "What do you want to know?"

"All about you," Matt said. "How you got into the business. Stuff like that."

Greg looked flattered. "Sure, I'll talk to you. Have a seat." Greg stood up and let Matt have his chair.

"Sure, kid. Ignore the rest of us," Sal teased.

As Matt sat down, he almost tumbled off—just like his uncle Ralph had. *Greg's chair was really low to the ground, probably because he was so tall. Interesting.*

Matt began his questions. Greg talked even more than Kenji, and he paced around the room, talking about how great he was and how great his ideas were. Finally Matt interrupted Greg.

"Hey, didn't I, um, see you near my uncle's office today?" he asked.

Greg frowned. "I don't think you did. I've been testing games all day. Right guys?" He turned to his fellow testers.

"All I know is that I'm about to beat level sixteen," Pete said, not taking his eyes off of the screen.

Matt stood up. "Well, thanks," he told Greg.

He hadn't learned much from Greg. But the whole chair thing stuck out in Matt's mind. He wouldn't cross Greg off his list of suspects yet.

Matt walked down the hallway, thoughts swirling in his head. Both Kenji and Greg had a reason to be mad at Ralph. He knew for sure that Kenji had been alone in Ralph's office. And Greg might have been there, too. But he couldn't prove for sure that either of them had messed with his uncle's computer and stolen the disks.

Lost in his thoughts, Matt bumped into Rachel coming in the opposite direction. She was carrying papers, which she dropped onto the floor.

"Sorry!" Matt said. He reached down to pick them up.

That's when he noticed the silver buttons on Rachel's skirt. *Just like the button he had found in Ralph's office.* He quickly glanced up and down the skirt and saw that one was missing. He remembered how Rachel had seemed unhappy with the way Uncle Ralph treated her. *Had Rachel gotten revenge on him?*

Matt handed the papers to Rachel. "Can I talk to you for my school report?" he asked. "I need to interview people to find out about their jobs."

94

Rachel nodded. "Come into my office."

Rachel's office was much smaller than Uncle Ralph's, but it was filled with video game posters and toys, too.

"I guess everyone around here loves video games," Matt remarked.

Rachel smiled. "Of course. That's why we work here."

Matt turned on the tape recorder. Rachel had a lot of interesting things to say.

"Lots of people don't think women can play or design video games as well as men can," she said. "I want to prove them wrong. I know I can be just as good as Kenji and Ralph."

"Are you mad that Uncle Ralph isn't helping you more?" Matt asked.

Rachel shrugged. "I can't make excuses. If I'm going to succeed, I've got to make it happen."

"So, I guess you're in my uncle's office all the time," Matt said.

"Yeah, I'm his assistant," Rachel pointed out. "Why'd you ask that?"

"No reason," Matt said quickly. "I'd better go. Thanks!"

TUESDAY, MARCH 14
3:32 P.M.

Matt sat at his uncle's desk, staring at the tape recorder. He felt like a failure. A tiny part of him had hoped that he could just get someone to confess into the tape recorder. But all he had were some lousy clues and a few suspects, but no real proof.

"Maybe I should listen again," Matt decided. He rewound the tape and played back the interviews, fast-forwarding over the boring parts.

Then he heard something. Something important.

Uncle Ralph walked in. He looked calmer, but he frowned when he saw Matt at his desk.

"I told you to stay away from my stuff," he said grumpily.

Matt pushed the tape recorder toward his uncle. "Listen to this," he said. "I know who fried your hard drive and stole your disks. And I can prove it!"

Can you solve the Case of the Super-Fried Hard Drive? Play Track 3 of the CD that came with your U-Solve-It! Mystery kit. You will hear excerpts from Matt's interviews with Kenji, Greg, and Rachel. Listen to the recordings carefully. See if you can figure out who fried Uncle Ralph's hard drive. Then check the U-Solve-It! web site to see if you're right!